LOL·A LEVINE

meets

JELLY

and

BEAN

MONICA BROWN

LOLA LEVINE

meets

JELLY and BEAN

ILLUSTRATED BY
Angela Dominguez

LITTLE, BROWN AND COMPANY
New York • Boston

Text copyright © 2017 by Monica Brown
Interior Artwork copyright © 2017 by Angela Dominguez
Yarn by Arthur Shlain

Cover design by Marcie Lawrence. Cover art copyright © 2017 by Angela Dominguez. Cover copyright © 2017 by Hachette Book Group, Inc.

Little, Brown and Company
Hachette Book Group
1290 Avenue of the Americas, New York, NY 10104
Visit us at lb-kids.com

First Edition: February 2017

Little, Brown and Company is a division of Hachette Book Group, Inc. The Little, Brown name and logo are trademarks of Hachette Book Group, Inc.

The publisher is not responsible for websites (or their content) that are not owned by the publisher.

ISBNs: 978-0-316-25853-1 (hardcover), 978-0-316-25850-0 (pbk.), 978-0-316-25852-4 (ebook)

Printed in the United States of America

LSC-C

10 9 8 7 6 5 4 3 2

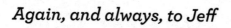

Again, and always, to Jeff

CONTENTS

Dear *Diario*,

The kitty-cat countdown starts today! School let out for the summer, so Dad says we finally have time to introduce a new pet to our family. Mom says we still have more to learn before we get our kitty, though. This Saturday, she is taking Ben and me to the library to find books about taking care of cats. I love going to the library, except when the librarians tell me to be quiet. I like to be *loud*. There's one librarian who I call Ms. Red because she has the reddest hair I've ever seen. She's my favorite. As long as there isn't anyone studying in the quiet zone, I can be as loud as I want. Well, maybe not as loud as I want, because that would be pretty loud, even for Ms. Red.

Sometimes, when I'm reading, I talk to the characters in my books. When I was little, I read a book called *Clara and the Curandera*. Mom explained that a *curandera* is a very wise woman. In the book, the *curandera* helps grumpy Clara become less grumpy. The nicer Clara is to everyone else, the happier she becomes. I cheer for her at the end of the book because I'm also trying to be less grumpy.

Especially when my soccer team,
the Orange Smoothies, loses
or when Alyssa Goldstein and
Makayla Miller tease me at school.
Luckily, it's summer, and I don't
need to see them much.

Meow! *¡Miau!*

Shalom,
Lola Levine

Chapter One
Mission Kitty-Cat

"¡Vámonos!" Mom says on Saturday morning. "Let's go!" We are going to the library to research cats so we know what to expect. Mom is humming as we get into the car. She always hums when she's happy. I

ask Mom a question I already know the answer to.

"Mom, why do you like libraries so much?"

"Because they are filled with books and people who love them," she says, smiling.

"You love books?" Ben asks.

"Yes," Mom says, "and I love the two of you."

During the summer, Mom takes us to the library on weekends, and we get lots and lots of books. Some kids check out one book at a time, but Ben and I check out as many as we can carry because morning is reading time. That's so Dad can go to his studio in the backyard and paint. Dad's an artist who works at home, and Mom works as a newspaper journalist. In the afternoon, it's swimming lessons, soccer in the park, or something creative in Dad's studio.

I wave at Ms. Red when we walk into the library, and she waves back. Mom helps us search for cat books on the computer in the children's section, and then we find the right row of books.

"Lola," she says, "I'm going to the adult section of the library. Can you watch your brother for ten minutes?"

"Okay," I say, and Ben and I start looking through the books. The problem is Ben doesn't like to do a lot of looking. Or sitting. He likes to do a lot of moving, and by that I mean jumping or dancing or kicking or climbing. His teacher told my parents that he's one of the most active kindergartners she's ever taught. She also said that Ben reminds her a lot of me at that age, whatever that means. After a few minutes of looking at books, I realize that Ben is gone. I can't find him anywhere until I hear a giggle from *above* me.

"Ben!" I say. "I'm supposed to be watching you! Get down. You are NOT allowed to climb on bookshelves." He ignores me until I say that I'm going to get Mom and Ms. Red.

"Okay, okay," he says, and gets ready to jump.

"Stop!" I say. "It's too high to jump! You'll get hurt, and I'll be the one to get in trouble. Do you want Mom to think we aren't ready to take care of a pet?! Just stay there." I walk over to the children's desk.

"Umm, is there a ladder or a stool I could use?" I ask Ms. Red.

"Do you need help reaching a book?" she asks.

"Not exactly..." I say, and then we both hear a loud crash. She follows me over to where Ben is now sitting on the floor, crisscross applesauce, acting like nothing happened. Except that the book he's pretending to read is upside down and he's trying to hide the other books that fell behind his back.

"Ben," I say, "that's it. I'm not letting you out of my sight." I help Ms. Red put the books back on the shelf, get my own

pile of books, and sit down right next to Ben. Then I tie one of Ben's shoelaces to one of mine so he can't move without me. Ms. Red smiles and goes back to her desk. Ben and I look at lots of books, and we each pick out our favorite. I choose *The Purrfect Guide to Cat Care*, and Ben chooses a book of cat jokes, which makes me roll my eyes.

"Lola, watch out or your eyes are going to get stuck that way—Mom said so," Ben says, sticking out his tongue. I am very happy when Mom gets back.

"Lola," she says, frowning, "why did you tie your shoelace to Ben's?"

"Don't even ask," I say. And she doesn't.

I read *The Purrfect Guide to Cat Care* all afternoon, and at dinner I start to list all the things we will need for a cat.

"We'll need a litter box, cat litter, food, bowls for food and fresh water, and best of all…we need a cat castle!" I say.

"What's that?" asks Dad.

"You know, a scratching post, a cat tree, a cat condo, a cat playground, a cat—"

"I get it now," says Dad. "Cats do need places to scratch and climb."

"We can buy one at the pet store or make one ourselves," I say, knowing which one Dad will choose.

"We'll make one!" Dad says happily. "It will be a fun project." Dad loves projects.

"Yes!" says Ben, who never met a hammer he didn't like. He helped Dad build a birdhouse last summer, which was great until he hammered one of his fingers. If people think I'm loud, they should hear Ben. It seemed like he yelled for an hour.

Luckily, there is a chapter on making your own cat castle in *The Purrfect Guide to Cat Care*. I make a list of the supplies we will need and give it to Dad.

Cat Castle Supplies

1. wood
2. sisal rope
3. natural carpet
4. cardboard tube
5. cat toys
6. screws, staples, and a whole bunch of different tools

(*note to Dad*—I know you will have what we need because you have everything there ever was in your studio.)

There's one thing on my list that confuses me, though.

"Dad," I ask, "what's sisal rope?" I know what rope is, but I've never heard of sisal rope before.

"It's a type of rope that's made from the agave plant in Mexico," Dad says. "I'll bet cats love it. You pronounce it like this: sigh-sull."

"Mexico?" I reply. "How cool! Wait until I tell Bella." Bella Benitez is my new super best friend, and her family is from Mexico. I bet she's seen an actual agave plant. My other super best friend is Josh Blot, who I've known my whole life, or at least it seems like it. Josh loves cats, just like me.

"What does an agave plant look like?" I ask Dad. Then he draws me one. It's pretty cool having a dad who is an artist.

Chapter Two
Frisbees and Sea Monsters

On Sunday afternoon, we go for a family bike ride. We bicycle past Josh's house and Bella's house because I want to leave them each a note. I like writing notes. And letters. And in my *diario*. When I grow up, I might be a journalist like my mom. I leave my note in Josh's mailbox. I see his cat, Milo, sitting in the window. I love Milo. When I visit Josh, Milo comes straight to me and slides around my ankles or sits on my lap. He has the softest fur I've ever felt, and I love the sound of his purr. Josh's mom, Principal Blot, says he's really old, so we need to be gentle with him. I think she's always a little surprised at how gentle I can be. Milo is why I want a pet cat.

Dear Josh,

Guess what?! We are getting a kitty in a few days. I'm so excited I can hardly sleep. Want to help us build a cat castle? How's your

cat, Milo? Maybe we can build one for him, too!

See you at swim lessons tomorrow!

Shalom,
Lola Levine

Then we bicycle over to Bella's house, and I slip a letter into her mailbox.

Dear Bella,

How are you?! How is ballet? I miss you! I'm so excited that you decided to take swim lessons with me and Josh. See you tomorrow. Yeah!

Shalom,
Lola Levine

P.S. I'm getting my kitty soon!

Finally, Mom, Dad, Ben, and I bicycle to the park and play Frisbee, which is really fun, until Ben throws the Frisbee up so high, it gets caught in a tree. A really tall one.

"Don't worry," I say. "This is a job for someone strong. I'll climb up the tree and get it."

"No, I'll get it." Ben says, racing me to the tree. We both start to climb as Mom and Dad reach us.

"Stop!" Dad says. "It's way too high for you to reach. Let me get it."

"Actually," Mom says, looking up at the tree, "I think you'll be too heavy for those branches. I can get it." Dad gives her a boost, and she climbs up the tree.

"Be careful, Mom!" I say, which is funny because that's what she usually says to me.

"Wow!" says Ben. "You could be a fireman, Mom, and save cats in trees!"

"Firewoman," says Dad. Mom climbs higher and higher, then stretches out her arms...and she reaches it! Mom grabs the Frisbee and tosses it down—I make a perfect catch, of course, because I am a goalie and that is what goalies do.

When Mom gets down from the tree, we all cheer and give her high fives! Who knew I had a mom who could climb trees?

"Is there anything you can't do, Mom?"
I ask.

"Yes," she says, laughing. "I can't get
all these leaves out of my hair by myself.
Help me, Lola."

The next afternoon, when we get to the aqua-plex, I'm wearing my new swimsuit because last year's suit is too small. I love my suit because it makes me look like I'm a scuba diver and it's black with orange stripes. Orange is one of my favorite colors, and it's the color of my soccer team, the Orange Smoothies. I see Bella right away because she is wearing a bright pink swimsuit with a little skirt, also pink. I don't like the color pink at all, but that's one opinion I've learned to keep to myself. Bella even wears a pink swim cap decorated with pink flowers. I don't wear a swim cap because my hair is short enough that it doesn't get in my way.

"Hi, Lola!" Bella says, giving me a hug. Bella likes to give hugs. I'm not used to this because before her all my friends were boys and they weren't big huggers. I hug her back.

"Hi, Bella!" I say. "What's new? Did you get my letter about the cat?"

"Yes! That's great," she says. And then we both see Josh walking toward us.

"Hi!" says Josh. I see his mom, Principal Blot, so I wave to her. I wonder if she misses me during the summer. It sure seems like I spend a *lot* of time with her during the school year, mostly by accident, like when Bella and I *accidentally* got into an ink fight while tie-dyeing our T-shirts for Spirit Week or when I *accidentally* hurt Juan Gomez on the soccer field. Principal Blot must not see me, though, because she doesn't wave back.

We are all pretty good swimmers, so

we spend each lesson practicing differ-ent strokes—today we focus on the back-stroke and the breaststroke. I like the breaststroke because I imagine I'm a frog swimming in a swamp looking for flies and insects to eat. I also dog-paddle in the water and ask the teacher why there isn't a cat paddle or a cat-stroke. She doesn't have an answer for me.

The really fun part comes after lessons when the three of us go to the water park connected to the pool. Ben meets us there. There are waterslides and fountains and a big ship to climb on—it's so much fun! I like water. It's so…refreshing. I like the sounds it makes when I stomp and splash and jump in like a cannonball. Luckily, Bella, Josh, and Ben do, too. We have a cannonball contest, and Bella wins! She makes the biggest splash, but her swim cap falls off, and I can see why she wears one. She has long ballerina hair that she wears in a bun to dance in.

"You look like a sea monster!" Ben says. I'm worried Bella will be upset, but she just laughs.

"I am a sea monster, and I am coming to get you, little fishy!" she says, sticking her arms out straight in front of her. That's how we make up our new game: sea monster attack! We take turns being the sea monster and the fish. Ben's sea monster is so crazy that the lifeguard walks over.

"Calm down, little dude," he says. "You're scaring the younger kids."

"Okay, big dude," says Ben.

That's my brother.

Chapter Three
The Cat Castle

A couple of days later, Dad takes Ben and me into his studio.

"It's time to lay down some plans for our cat play structure."

"You mean our cat castle," says Ben. "Why do the plans need to lie down?"

"I mean to say that we should put our design ideas down on paper," Dad says.

"Oh," Ben says, still looking confused.

I grab a piece of paper and a pencil.

"Ben," I say, "just draw what you'd like our cat castle to look like."

"Exactly," says Dad, "but we might not have room for an actual castle—maybe just a cat condo."

"Okay," says Ben. Then we all sit around sketching. After we are done, we present our designs to Dad.

"Wow," says Dad. "These are very creative ideas. But I'm not sure we can do all of this." He looks at our two drawings and then starts sketching his own.

We see Dad's final drawing, which
includes some of Ben's ideas and some of
mine.

"I love it!" says Ben.

"Perfect!" I say.

"Great!" says Dad. "Let's go to the hard-
ware store and pick up some supplies."

The rest of the week, whenever we aren't reading or at swim lessons, we work on our cat castle. I also remember that I have to protect my goldfish, Mia, named after the amazing soccer player Mia Hamm. Dad helps me put metal mesh over the goldfish bowl so my new kitty won't bother her.

Our cat castle turns out great! Mom even helps me sew a pillow shaped like a bird to dangle from the top. Our kitty will love it! Dad has to keep reminding Ben that the cat castle is for a ten-pound cat, not a five-year-old boy, and that no, he *can't* climb on it. We finish the cat castle on Friday night, which is a good thing, because tomorrow, on Saturday, we are getting our kitty! Of course, the night before, I'm much too excited to sleep. My mind is doing jumping jacks. I decide to write in my diary.

Dear *Diario*,

Tomorrow is the big day! After waiting and waiting and hoping and asking, we are finally going to get a KITTY! Right after breakfast, we are going to go to the animal shelter and pick out my very first furry pet! Mom always tells me that I have lots of love to give, and I can't wait to give it to my new pet. Last night, I took down the picture I drew of a kitty that hangs on the wall over my bed, because pretty soon I will have a real kitty to play with.

Shalom,
Lola Levine

After I finish writing in my *diario*, I still can't sleep. So I start thinking of cat names. I start with *A* names: Albert...Abby... Ava...Addie...Adam. Then I move on to the *B*s: Boris...Barney...Bee...Beth....

Chapter Four
The Big Day

When we all arrive at Another Chance Animal Shelter, Ben and I scramble out of the car and start to run to the front door.

"Stop!" Mom says. "You know better than to run in the parking lot. Be careful."

"Sorry!" I say, and turn back to grab her hand as we walk together into the shelter. Dad lifts Ben and puts him on his shoulders.

"Why is this place called Another Chance?" Ben asks.

"Because Another Chance is a shelter that gives a home to animals that don't have a family to live with," Dad explains.

"What happens if they don't find a home with a family?" Ben asks with a frown.

"They can live here forever," Dad says, smiling.

We walk through the doors and see a sign that says ALL ANIMALS DESERVE A GOOD LIFE.

I read it out loud for Ben.

"All people deserve a good life, too, right?" Ben says, tugging Dad's hair.

34

"Yep," I say, "and I bet people who are nice to pets are nice to people, too."

"That's right, wise one," Mom says.

"Don't you have to be old to be wise?" I ask Mom, wondering if she's joking.

"No," Mom answers. "Wise just means smart with a little kindness thrown in."

We see a girl sitting behind a welcome desk. Her name tag says HI! I'M ZOE! and she has a ring—through her nose! It's gold. We sit down, and I say, "We are here to adopt a kitty!"

Zoe asks us lots of questions and reminds us that kitties need cool fresh water, food, playtime, and respect. I tell her that I know how to scoop, dump, and clean a litter box, and then Ben interrupts.

"I won't clean the litter box, but I'll be

feeding the kitty and giving her water!" he says.

"That's because he throws up easily," I explain, remembering the time he threw up in a garbage can outside my classroom. We were doing a composting project, and there were a lot of wiggly worms involved.

My parents fill out a bunch of forms, and then Zoe says, "Do you have any questions for me?"

"Yes," I say. "How do you blow your nose with that ring in there?"

"Lola!" Mom and Dad say at the same time.

"Be polite," Dad says.

Zoe doesn't seem to mind, though. She looks at me, smiles, and says, "Very carefully."

I like Zoe. We follow her down the hall toward the kitty room, when suddenly Ben says, "I've got to pee!"

"Just wait, Ben," I say. "I want to pick out our kitty!"

"But the doctor says it's not good to wait," Ben says, and does a little hop. I roll my eyes.

"I've got an idea," says Dad. "I'll take Ben to the restroom, and we'll meet you in the kitty room."

"Good plan," says Mom. We follow Zoe to the young cat room and see all sorts of kitties. They are all so cute and cuddly I wonder how I'll ever decide. Then I feel something furry slide around my ankles and calves. I look down to see an orange cat with the greenest eyes I've ever seen.

"What a beauty," Mom says, carefully picking up the cat. "She or he is friendly, too!"

"Can I hold her?" I ask Mom. The cat looks young but not quite a kitten.

"Of course!" Mom says, and hands her to me. She looks at the tag on the orange kitty's collar and walks over to the bulletin board.

"This kitty is a girl, and she's nine months old," Mom says, "and great with kids. Her owners had to move to a place that doesn't allow cats."

I hold the orange cat in my arms and gently run my hands over her fur. She purrs.

"I don't think you need to pick out a

cat," says Zoe. "I think your cat picked you!"

"I agree," says Mom. "She is one sweet kitty."

We are already back in the front of the shelter with our new orange kitty when Dad and Ben find us.

"There you are!" says Dad.

"We got distracted by the puppies," says Ben. "Is this our new cat?"

"We hope so!" I say. "Mom and I think she's perfect. We are just waiting to see what you think."

Ben walks up to me and carefully pets the orange kitty.

"She's amazing. I didn't know cats could be that *orange*," he says. "Can we keep her?"

"We sure can," Dad answers.

On the way home from Another Chance Animal Shelter, we debate names for our new pet.

"We could call her Sunny, because she's orange," I say, but it doesn't quite seem right.

"How about Cheddar?!" says Ben. "Or Cheese Puff?"

"I really don't think her name needs to be cheese-related," I say.

"Carrot?" suggests Ben. "Mango?"

"Why are all your suggestions food?" I ask.

"Because I am soooooooooooooo hungry!" says Ben.

"We'll make you some sandwiches when we get home," Dad says.

We slowly introduce our not-so-little kitty to her new home. She seems to like it. After a while, Dad brings in some peanut butter and grape jelly sandwiches—my favorite. They are shaped like stars and hearts. Dad believes in "creative expression," even with food. He says it's not wasteful because he eats the crusts after he cuts out the shapes. Mom brings us tall glasses of *chicha morada*, our favorite drink from Peru. That's where Tía Lola, the aunt I'm named for, lives and where my mom grew up. *Chicha morada* is made from purple corn that's cooked with spices and pineapple and then poured over ice, but it looks just like grape juice. Mom uses instant *chicha morada* packs Tía Lola sends her from Lima, Peru. I like stirring the purple powder into the water.

"When I was little, my mother would boil the purple corn with cinnamon sticks, sugar, cloves, and pineapple," Mom says, taking a big drink.

"Tell me more stories about Peru," I tell Mom. I went to Peru with my parents when I was only two and my brother was a baby, but I don't remember much.

"Well, my mom is one of nine children, and my father is one of five, so Lola and I always had lots of cousins to play with."

"I wish I had cousins to play with," I say. Dad is an only child, and Tía Lola doesn't have children.

"Well," says Mom, "now you have Ben AND your new cat to play with."

"I know," I say, smiling. I also have my two super best friends, Josh and Bella.

"Lola!" Ben yells. "Look! The kitty is licking the grape jelly off your plate. She likes it!"

"She does," I say, taking away the plate. I reach to pet her, and she licks my fingers. It feels scratchy.

"Do you like jelly?" I ask. She purrs, and I have an idea. "What if we name her Jelly?"

"I like that," says Dad.

"Me too," says Mom.

"Ben?" I ask.

"Jelly…Jelly…," Ben says, concentrating on something. "You know…grape jelly is purrrple!" Ben says. "Get it? Purrrple?"

"Yes!" I say. "We have a winner! Welcome to our family, Jelly Levine!"

Chapter Five
The Polka-Dot Ghost

Later, we are playing in my bedroom when Jelly walks over and sits in Ben's lap.

"Hi, Jelly!" says Ben, but then he starts sniffling. I look at Ben and realize something is wrong. His eyes are watery, and it looks like he's trying to hold something in because his face is all red and scrunched up.

"Ben, do you have to go to the bathroom?" I ask. He shakes his head.

"Are you going to throw up?" I say, and now I'm really worried. Ben shakes his head. Then suddenly his mouth opens, and he lets out a great big loud—

"Achoooooooooooooo!"

And then he sneezes again. And again. And he doesn't stop.

"Achoooooooooooooo! Achoooooooooo! Achoooooooooooooo! Achoooooooooo!"

I'm thinking I should get Mom when he finally has enough breath to say, "Get Jelly away from me!"

"What?!" I say, scooping Jelly into my

arms. "What did Jelly ever do to you?" Still, I open the door of my bedroom and let Jelly out. I think she's scared of Ben's sneezing, so she's happy to go.

"I think Jelly makes me sneeze," Ben says, wiping his nose and eyes. "I was okay before I played with her."

Oh no! I think. Not that!

"Maybe you just have a cold...," I say.

"But I don't," Ben says.

"I think you just have a cold," I say a little louder. Ben just looks confused. "Ben," I continue, "do you know what will happen if you are allergic to Jelly?"

"No," he says, "what?"

"THEY WILL TAKE HER AWAY!" I say.

"But I love Jelly!" says Ben, and now his eyes are watering for another reason.

"I know," I say. "So, Ben, I have a question for you. Are you getting a cold?"

"No. I mean, yes! I am. I really am." Then he fake coughs and says, "I have a fever I think. I need to tell Mom to buy Popsicles and make chicken soup and—"

"Ben! Don't overdo it, or Mom and Dad will know you are faking. And try to stay away from Jelly."

"I will," he says, looking pretty miserable.

The next morning, I wake up to the sound of Ben yelling. It's coming from the direction of his room. I run across the hall, followed by Mom and Dad.

"I'm covered in dots!" Ben says, and he is. He has bumpy things all over his face and arms. "Help!"

"*Benito*," Mom says, "what's wrong? When did this happen to your skin?"

"They almost look like bug bites," Dad says, "but none of us have them. I don't think these are from mosquitoes."

"Maybe he's allergic to something," Mom says. "They look a lot like hives."

"Hives! What's that?" Ben asks, and starts to cry. "Does this have something to do with bees? My bumps itch!"

"It's okay, Ben," Dad says. "We'll take you to the doctor. These hives have nothing to do with bees. But I wonder what you are allergic to? What did you eat yesterday?"

I look at Ben, and I feel so bad I could almost cry. I take a big breath.

"He's allergic to Jelly," I say. "He was sneezing each time he got near her last night." Mom and Dad don't look very happy.

"Why didn't you tell us, Ben?" Dad asks, but he's looking at me.

"It's my fault," I say, and then the rest comes out. "I told Ben to pretend he has a cold."

"Lola," Mom says, "I am very disappointed in you—first for not telling us the truth and second for encouraging Ben to ignore how his body feels."

"I think you need to go to your room now, Lola," Dad says. Mom nods her head.

"I'm sorry, Lola," Ben says, still crying.

"I'm the one who is sorry," I say, and go to my room.

I lie down on my bed. My tummy hurts like it does when I do something wrong. I decide to write Mom and Dad a note, and I give it to Mom when she brings me some toast and hot milk with honey for breakfast.

Dear Mom and Dad,

I am so sorry I didn't tell you about Ben. It's just that I have wanted a pet for so long, and I love Jelly so much that I didn't want her to go away. But I know that lying is never okay, and I promise I won't do it again. I especially won't do it again if it means Ben will get sick and then get covered in dots and look even weirder than he already does. I really hope the dots go away.

Shalom,
Lola Levine

Then I write another note for Ben, who is still at the doctor with Dad.

Dear Ben,

I'm sorry I told you to lie. I hope you didn't get in trouble, too.

Lola

P.S. I love you even more than I love Jelly, so I guess I'll be okay.

Luckily, Ben comes back from the doctor feeling much better, and my parents tell me to come downstairs for lunch. I give Ben my note, and my dad says that everyone makes mistakes and it's okay as long as we learn from them. Ben is still covered in dots, but now they are pink and even bigger.

"The doctor gave me medicine, and I'm wearing lotion that stops the hives from itching!" he says. "It smells funny and makes me look like a polka-dot ghost! The doctor says the hives will go away soon now that—"

"Now that what?" I say.

"Now that Jelly is staying in Dad's studio," he says.

"Only until we can find her a good home," says Dad.

"But what if we CAN'T find Jelly a good home?" I ask Dad.

"Then Jelly has to go back to the shelter," Dad says.

"But I'm going to ask around at work," Mom says.

"And Dad says we can make adopt-a-kitty posters and put them up at the rec center," says Ben.

"And around the neighborhood...," says Mom.

"Okay," I say.

I go visit Jelly in Dad's studio. It's not too hot or too cold, and my dad set up the cat castle there. He also made sure anything that might be dangerous for cats was locked away in his big metal closet. Still, I think Jelly looks lonely. And I really don't like the fact that she will sleep alone at night. We play for a long time, and then I go to my room. When my dad comes in later, my head is resting on my folded arms on my desk and I'm crying.

"Hi, Lola," Dad says. "Are you still thinking about Jelly?"

"Yes," I say. "I don't want to stop because what if I never see Jelly again and I forget her? I'll be sad forever."

"You won't forget her, Lola," he says. "I promise."

"You're right, Dad," I say, raising my head and looking at him. I notice that he has splatters of paint on his cheek and on his T-shirt. This is nothing new since he's always painting. It gives me an idea.

"I know," I say. "I'll paint a picture of Jelly and put it on my wall."

"That's a great idea!" says Dad. "I

think you should use watercolors this time. Let's go get some special paper from my studio."

"I agree," I say, and I'm glad my dad is an artist. Creative expression is a good thing, in my opinion. I paint a picture of Jelly and finish just before bedtime. It's hard for me to fall asleep—but not because I'm excited. I can't sleep because I'm sad. I try to think of nice things, like ice cream, soccer, my goldfish Mia, Tía Lola, and my *bubbe*. It doesn't really work because I really can't stop thinking about Jelly.

Chapter Six
Adopt a Kitty

"Lola, I have a surprise for you," Mom says the next morning, peeking her head into my room. She's about to leave for work.

"What's the surprise?" I ask.

"I brought you your favorite people,"

she says, and walks into my room, followed by Bella and Josh.

"Yeah!" I say. I'm so happy to see them.

"We heard about Jelly," says Bella.

"And we want to help," says Josh.

"I hope you can," I say. "I need to make lots of ADOPT A KITTY posters. I'm going to put them up everywhere."

"Let's do it together, Lola!" Bella says.

"You three get to spend the day together," Mom says. "Then Dad will take all of you to swim lessons this afternoon. Ben is spending the day at Mira's house."

Mira is Ben's best friend. I like her a lot, even if her sister *is* Alyssa Goldstein. The last time I saw Alyssa, she told me that I was weird. Luckily, I have my two super best friends who don't think I'm weird. Or if they do, they don't seem to care. I give Mom a hug good-bye.

"You are the best mom in the whole wide world," I whisper in her ear.

"And you are the best daughter in the whole wide world," she whispers back.

"Is this Jelly?" asks Bella, looking at the new painting on my wall.

"It sure is," I say. "Want to meet her?"

"Definitely!" Josh says.

"Yes!" says Bella.

I lead them to Dad's studio, and we take Jelly outside with a leash and some of her cat toys. We play with Jelly for a long time. She pounces and rolls around and purrs.

"She's an awesome cat," says Josh. "Somebody will want to adopt her for sure."

"I wish I could," says Bella, "but I already asked my parents, and they said no because we travel to Mexico so much."

"And I've already got Milo," Josh says. "I don't think my mom would let me have two cats." Josh is right—his mom seems to say no a lot.

"We need to find a super-awesome somebody to adopt Jelly," I say, "and that's that!" My *bubbe*, Grandma Levine, says "That's that!" a lot, and I like it. She has lots of opinions, just like me, and when she says something, she means it.

"I agree," says Josh. The three of us go back upstairs to make lots of ADOPT A KITTY posters, and then I ask Dad if we can put them up around the neighborhood.

"Sure," he says. "As long as you stick

together, look both ways before you cross the street, and be back before lunchtime. And don't go any farther than Josh's house."

"And Jelly—" I say, but Dad interrupts.

"I promise to play with her," Dad says and pats my shoulder.

It's bright and sunny outside, and by the time we finish putting up posters, we are hot and tired.

"Want to stop by my house for some lemonade?" says Josh.

"Yes!" says Bella, and I agree. When we get to Josh's house, his mom is in the backyard garden. It seems like she's always there when I visit during the

summer. Maybe it's because she has to be in an office all day during the school year.

"Hi, Principal Blot," I say. Josh's cat, Milo, comes up to me and says hello. Even though he's big and slow, he still reminds me a little of Jelly.

"Hi, Milo," I say. "I thought I'd have a pet cat, just like you, but it turns out that my brother is allergic."

"Your mom told me about Jelly," Principal Blot says, and stands up. "I'm sorry to hear it."

"She's in my dad's art studio for now," I say, and suddenly I feel like crying. "But if we don't find a family for her soon, we have to take her back to the shelter, because cats and paint don't go together and Dad needs to work. We'd better get back. It's almost lunchtime, and I think Jelly gets bored in there."

"Wait, I have an idea," Principal Blot says, and walks over to the corner of her garden. She bends over and snips off a few leaves. "Here's some fresh catnip, Lola. Jelly will love it. Rub it on her scratching post and her cat toys, and she'll be really entertained."

"Thanks!" I say, and I can't wait to get home with my gift for Jelly. I didn't know Principal Blot could be so nice.

"Mom!" says Josh. "I almost forgot! We made these ADOPT A KITTY posters for Jelly." He gives one to his mom. "Can you put this up at school? I know the students are gone, but teachers still come by." Principal Blot nods and takes a look at our poster.

"Oh, she's an orange tabby," says

Principal Blot, smiling. "How lovely. I had an orange tabby when I was a little girl. We called her Marmalade."

When we get home, we eat lunch and then introduce Jelly to catnip. She loves it! She's so fun to watch. After swim lessons and the water park, I am so tired. When I get home, I make an announcement.

"I, Lola Levine, am taking a nap."

"Wow," says Dad. "I don't think I've ever heard you say those words together."

"No way!" says Ben. He's still covered in white splotches, but they are much less bumpy.

"Good for you," says Mom, who is

home early from work. "You've had an emotional few days," she says. "Ben's going to the grocery store with Dad, so the house will be quiet."

"Are you saying I can't be quiet?" asks Ben.

"Well," I say, "can you?"

"Probably not," he admits. "Mrs. Goldstein asked me to keep my voice down more than once today. Finally, she just told Mira and me to go play in the backyard."

I go upstairs to lie down, but before I do, I write a quick note in my *diario*.

Dear *Diario,*

I'm worried we won't find a home for Jelly. I know that she will be okay at the shelter, but I want her to have a family of her very own to love. Mom says to be patient, but I just don't know how I can do that. It's like trying to keep my foot still with a soccer ball touching my toe. Besides, patience just means waiting and waiting, and, in my opinion, waiting isn't fun at all. Especially when my kitty is all by herself in my dad's studio. Maybe my parents will let me sleep out there with Jelly tonight. I can bring my sleeping bag. I'm going to close my eyes now because I'm getting pretty tired of them leaking.

Shalom,
Lola Levine

When I wake up, I smell…pancakes!

"Hi, Lola!" Dad says. "We are having breakfast for dinner. What shape pancakes do you want?" My dad is so silly.

"How about a great big smiley face?" I say. I love breakfast for dinner, and I need to cheer up.

"I want a monster!" says Ben.

"Surprise me," says Mom, who is making us banana milk shakes without the ice cream.

"Want to help Ben make scrambled eggs?" Dad says, smiling. Since Ben making just about anything alone can be pretty dangerous, I agree. Ben gets a little crazy whipping the eggs with a fork and makes a mess, but other than that, our eggs turn out great—and green, because Mom chops up some spinach and makes us swirl it in.

Dad makes a big heart-shaped pancake for Mom and a blob he calls a monster for Ben, but my smiley face is perfect.

We are just finishing clearing the table when the doorbell rings.

"I'll get it," says Dad, and he practically skips to the door.

"Why is Dad so bouncy?" I ask Mom. "I mean his pancake art did turn out good, but…"

"I think it might have to do with your second surprise today," Mom says.

"I get ANOTHER surprise?" I say.

"Yep!" says Ben, and he starts hopping

up and down. Dad walks in the house with none other than … Principal Blot!

"Hi, Lola," she says, and she's smiling. I still can't get used to it.

"What are you doing here?" I ask.

"Well…," Principal Blot says, "Josh and I had a long talk today, and we both think we have room for another cat at our house. Will you introduce me to Jelly?"

I'm so surprised that I can't move or even say anything. I just stare at Principal Blot with my mouth open, that is, until Ben gives me a push.

"Lola!" he says. "This means you will be able to visit her! And Jelly will have a big brother cat, Milo!"

"Shall we go to the studio?" Dad says, smiling at me.

"Yes!" I say, and when we get to the studio, I do something I've never, ever done before. I run to Principal Blot and give her a great big hug.

Dear *Diario*,

Guess what? Tonight was the best night ever. Principal Blot loved Jelly. And Jelly loved her back. I can't believe my kitty is going to be adopted by my super best friend! And Principal Blot may be a little scary as a principal, but she sure isn't as a cat mom! Double yeah! And now I'll know that Jelly is just a few blocks away, with a garden full of catnip!

Tonight, before I go to sleep, I'm going to think of all the words that mean happy because that's what I am. Happy! And glad... cheerful...jolly...excited...smiling... super-duper...awesome...*feliz*... *alegre*!

Shalom,
Lola Levine

Chapter Seven
The Last Surprise

My week is very weird. It seems like Dad and Ben go off and disappear together a lot, but I don't mind because I get to go over to Josh's house and visit Milo and Jelly whenever I want. They are so cute

together. Milo doesn't seem to mind that Jelly always wants to play, and Josh says Milo needs the exercise.

"I'm so happy you adopted Jelly Levine," I say to Principal Blot. "I'll bet you never thought you'd have a Levine in your family!"

"I sure didn't," she replies, and bends down to pet Jelly, who purrs and nuzzles Principal Blot's hand. Josh is super-duper happy, too. His house is a little quiet sometimes because he doesn't have any brothers or sisters, and his dad lives in another town. Jelly keeps him busy! He moved our giant cat castle into his room, so he gets to watch the cats play and scratch and climb all the time.

One day, a few weeks later, I'm in my room reading when I hear Ben yell.

"Lola! Zola! Granola!" he says. "Come out into the backyard for a picnic. Mom's home for lunch!"

"Yeah!" I think. I love it when Mom comes home for lunch. Usually she is so busy investigating or interviewing or writing stories for the newspaper that she has to eat lunch at her desk. I hop down the stairs two at a time and don't see anyone in the kitchen. They must be outside already.

As soon as I walk into the backyard, I see something move—a fluffy little bundle of black fur with a spot of white on his chest. A little black puppy is running around the yard sniffing everything he can.

"He's a boy!" says Ben. I kneel on the grass, and the black puppy runs over to me. I give him a hug and then look at Ben to check for dots. He reads my mind.

"Dad and I have been going to the shelter every day, so I can play with the dogs and make sure I'm not allergic."

"Is he ours?" I ask. I can hardly believe it.

"He's ours," Dad says, and I start crying. Again! I've cried more in the last month than I have since I was two. Our new puppy licks my chin and then he's off and running. He is the cutest puppy I've ever seen.

"So do you like him?" asks Mom.

"I LOVE him!" I say. I pick up the red ball that's on the ground and toss it toward him. He scrambles to get it and fit it into his little mouth. "What's his name?" I ask.

"I had an idea," says Ben. "I thought we could name him Bean in honor of Jelly. You know, because jelly and bean sort of go together—like candy. And then his two names will rhyme."

"That's true," I say, laughing. "I like it! Welcome to the family, Bean Levine."

"Yeah!" Mom says.

"Family hug!" says Dad.

"Yes!" I say. "But not without Bean!"

"Lola, I've got a joke for you," Ben says. "Why do dogs run in circles?"

"Why?" I say.

"Because it's hard to run in squares!"

Chapter Eight
Woof

During the summer, we go to the library on the weekends, and we get lots and lots of books. Some kids check out one book at a time, but Ben and I check out as many as we can carry because every morning is reading time. This time, we are looking at books about how to build the perfect doghouse!

"Hi, Ms. Red!" I say when Mom, Ben, and I walk into the children's section of the library. Then I stop. I said that out loud, and I don't actually know Ms. Red's real name.

"I'm sorry," I say. "That's the name I call you in my head because of your pretty red hair. I don't know your real name." I hope she won't be mad.

"That's okay," she says. "Red is my favorite color."

"What's your real name?" I ask.

"Ruby," she says, smiling.

"I'm pretty sure I can remember that!" I say, and then we laugh together.

Dear *Diario,*

It's been a crazy summer. First I
got a cat and was happy. Then
I found out my brother, Ben, is
allergic to cats, and I was sad.
I learned two things. One, you
should NEVER lie about how
your body feels, and two, having
friends and the best family in the
whole wide world can make you
feel better. I was worried that I
wouldn't find an awesome home
for my cat, Jelly Levine, but then
I did! I was happy again. I didn't
think things could get any better,
but then I found out they could.
I now have a new puppy named

Bean Levine. He is amazing. And guess what? It's taken us a long time, but I think he's finally potty trained. Yeah!

Shalom,
Lola Levine

P.S. Woof! Woof! *¡Guau! ¡Guau!*